To Justin, with all my love,

Emma xx

With thanks to the boys of Lanesborough School

A TEMPLAR BOOK

First published in the UK in 2007 by Templar Publishing,
an imprint of The Templar Company plc,
Pippbrook Mill, London Road, Dorking, Surrey, RH4 1JE, UK
www.templarco.co.uk

First edition

ISBN 978-1-84011-980-0

Edited by Libby Hamilton

Printed in Singapore

I THOUGHT I SAW A DINOSAUR!

Emma Dodd

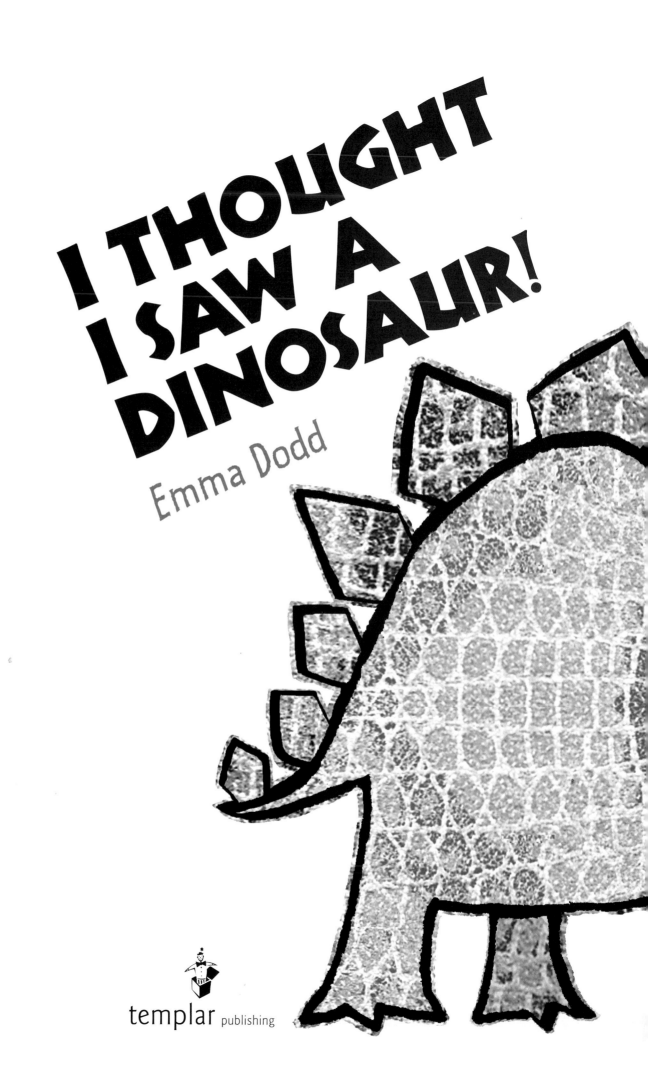

templar publishing

Jack and his cousins, Olly and Issy,
were camping in the garden.

"Let's hunt for **DINOSAURS**," said Jack.

"Alright," said Jack's mum.
"Don't get too scared."

When it was dark, they tiptoed down the path and into the woods at the bottom of the garden.

The woods were very dark and creepy.

WHOOOOOOO!

"It's a dinosaur!" squeaked Olly.
A huge shape loomed
over them.

"No, **look** – it's only an owl!" laughed Issy.

"We weren't **really** scared," said Jack and Olly.

They crept along the path,
through the trees.

Green eyes stared at them.
"It's a dinosaur!" hissed Jack.

MRROOOWWL!

"No, look – it's only a cat!" giggled Issy.

Eeeeeeek!

Suddenly everything was
still and silent.

"Where's Issy?"
asked Jack.

They ran back to the tent
as fast as they could.

"There's... there's...
there's **something**
in the tent!" shrieked Issy.

"It's my **mum!**" laughed Jack.

"I wasn't really scared," said Issy,
turning a little pink.

Jack's mum had brought hot chocolate for them.
"Come on," she said, "it's time for bed now.
Sleep well you three. See you in the morning."

"I knew there weren't
any dinosaurs," said Issy sleepily.

"Me too," yawned Olly.

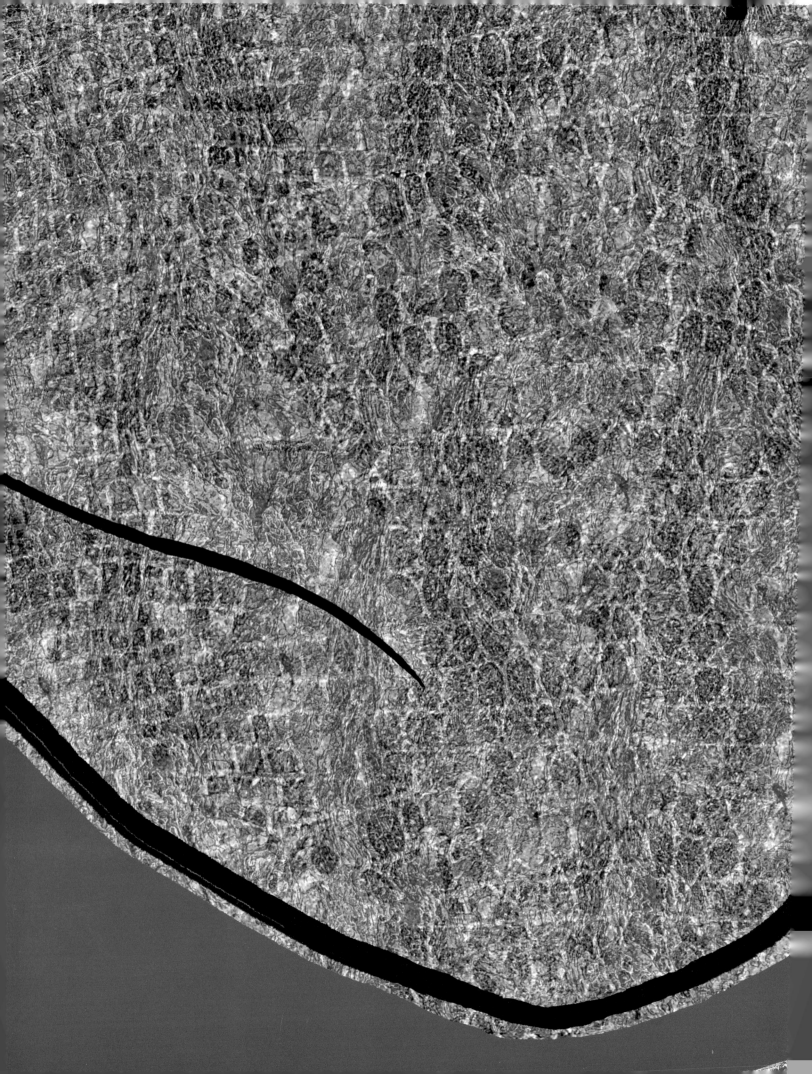

"I'm not so sure," said Jack.
But the others were
already asleep.